The Best C

in the world

Written and Illustrated by
Marta Cappa
Copyright 2010
Updated and Reprinted 2012
By Marta Cappa

Published by Marta Cappa

For my boys. Thanks for loving my stories!

For additional copies and information, please visit:
www.StoriesFromSlumberVillage.com.

Requests for permission to make copies of any part of the work should be submitted online at Marta@StoriesFromSlumberVillage.com.

Library of Congress Cataloging-in-Publication Data:
Cappa, Marta
Stories from Slumber Village
The Best Grandpa in the World

Hall of Fame

Rowdy's Grandpa Buck is the best grandpa in Slumber Village.

Whenever they are together, they have fun.
On sunny days, they go fishing. Rowdy likes to catch big fish.
Grandpa likes to catch the little ones.

On stormy days, they play checkers. Rowdy likes to win.
Grandpa doesn't care. He likes to be with Rowdy.

On lazy days, they play hide and seek. Rowdy likes to hide.
Grandpa likes to seek. And then Grandpa likes to take a nap.

On cloudy days, they run races. Rowdy likes to hurry. Grandpa likes to take his time. Eventually, they both finish. Rowdy thinks that Grandpa Buck is the best grandpa in Slumber Village.

But, someone disagreed. One day, Rowdy's friend, Jinx, said, "My grandpa is the best in Slumber Village." Rowdy didn't believe her.

Jinx continued. "My grandpa is the best because he was an astronaut." Rowdy was impressed. "Oh, my!" he said. He had always wanted to go to the moon.

Jinx told more stories about her grandpa. "My grandpa was an Eagle
Scout," she boasted, "and he saved a group of lost hikers once. All. . .
by. . . himself!" Rowdy was tired of hearing her stories. He was not
impressed anymore. He said, "Oh, no." He wanted to turn off his ears.

Jinx had more stories to tell. "My grandpa is strong.
He wrestled a bear one time . . . and won!" It reminded Rowdy of the
time his grandpa fought some moles in the back yard. He was going to
tell her about it, but it didn't seem very dangerous. And besides, the moles
won. Rowdy said, "Oh, brother!"

And oh, how he wished his grandpa had won. Grandpa didn't seem so great
after all.

During the long walk home,
Rowdy's thoughts drifted
back to Grandpa Buck.

"*The girl in the red cape, blah, blah, blah. Big bad wolf, blah, blah, blah. Grandma safe.... The End.*"

Rowdy was disappointed. Grandpa Buck's bedtime stories are terrible. When Grandpa reads a story, he leaves parts out, it takes about 30 seconds, and then Grandpa falls asleep.

Rowdy's grandpa always needs help with puzzles.

And when he makes Rowdy breakfast, it's always a stinky, sticky bowl of something Grandpa Buck calls gruel! Eww!

And the worst of it, Grandpa Buck can't even work the TV! If Rowdy had to depend on him, he'd never get to see his favorite shows. It was really getting hard for Rowdy to remember anything fun about Grandpa Buck. He was starting to think he might like to get a new one.

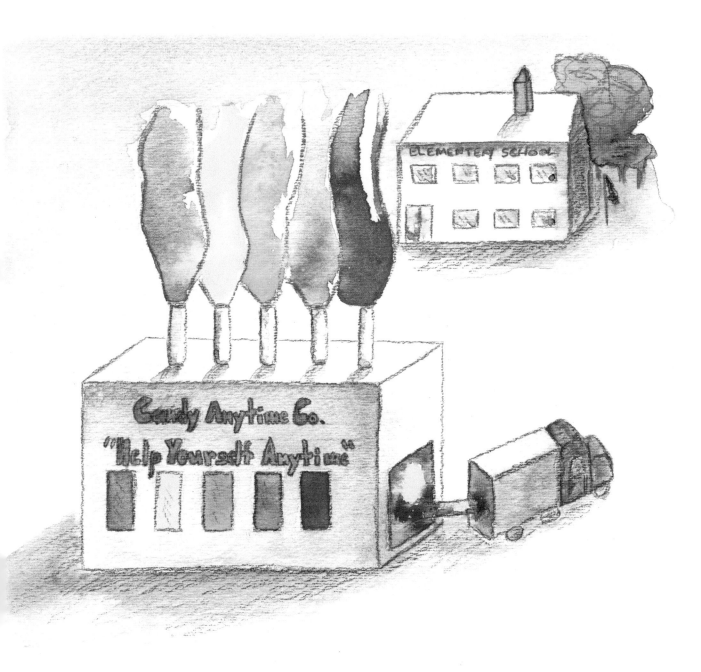

Rowdy thought that if he could invent the best grandpa, the new and improved one would take him to school in a hot air balloon.

His grandpa would own a candy factory. And Rowdy would get candy even when his mom and dad would say no.

And Grandpa would have a super hero cape in his closet just in case of emergencies. He'd be the best grandpa ever.

On Saturday, Rowdy's mom said Grandpa Buck was coming to visit. Rowdy wasn't looking forward to it. Well, maybe just a little bit. He didn't feel like having fun, but he hoped he would. What could Grandpa Buck possibly do that would be better than wrestling a bear?

That morning, Grandpa Buck built Rowdy a tree house. Rowdy noticed Grandpa liked to build, and he liked what Grandpa built.

Then, Grandpa Buck took Rowdy for a long walk on the beach. Grandpa liked to poke and dig in the sand. Rowdy liked to stand back and watch. "Grandpa, you sure know how to find all the best stuff that washes up on the sand," he said.

After that, Grandpa Buck taught Rowdy how to fly a kite. Rowdy taught Grandpa how to get the kite out of the tree. They were having fun.

It was getting late in the afternoon. Rowdy was tired. Grandpa wanted to walk. Rowdy wanted a ride. Grandpa lifted Rowdy to his shoulders. Rowdy felt like he was riding a giant. He could see everything from up there.

Grandpa even took him out for ice cream. Rowdy ordered chocolate.
Grandpa ordered chocolate vanilla swirl. They both ordered doubles.

That night, Grandpa was too tired to read Rowdy a story. Rowdy was too tired to hear one. Instead, Grandpa Buck gave Rowdy a big bear hug and said, "Rowdy, you're my best friend."

That was the best day of Rowdy's life.

The next day, Rowdy told Jinx that he had the best grandpa ever. Jinx said, "Oh, my! The best?"

"The best grandpa in the world!" Rowdy shouted.
He told her all about Grandpa Buck.

Just then, another boy arrived. He had been listening to Rowdy's stories about Grandpa Buck. The boy said, "That's nothing. You should hear about my grandpa. He's great. He's an inventor. He invented the . . ."

But Rowdy and Jinx didn't hear what he invented. They weren't listening. They were wondering. . . could there possibly be three best grandpas in Slumber Village? Well, could there?

And that is how Grandpa Buck
became one of the best grandpas
~~in Slumber Village.~~

in the world!

Stories from Slumber Village is readily available on line at
www.StoriesFromSlumberVillage.com
www.Amazon.com
or from your favorite online bookseller.

You can also special order copies from your neighborhood book store.

Please tell your friends about these wonderful stories. If you become a fan on Face Book, you will have access to the **coloring pages.**

Visit www.facebook.com/storiesfromslumbervillage or my website for more information.

45364621R00024

Made in the USA
Charleston, SC
18 August 2015